Melmoth Reconciled

Honoré de Balzac

Translated by Ellen Marriage

MELMOTH RECONCILED

By Honore De Balzac

Translated by Ellen Marriage

To Monsieur le General Baron de Pommereul, a token of the friendship
between our fathers, which survives in their sons.

DE BALZAC.

MELMOTH RECONCILED

There is a special variety of human nature obtained in the Social Kingdom by a process analogous to that of the gardener's craft in the Vegetable Kingdom, to wit, by the forcing-house—a species of hybrid which can be raised neither from seed nor from slips. This product is known as the Cashier, an anthropomorphous growth, watered by religious doctrine, trained up in fear of the guillotine, pruned by vice, to flourish on a third floor with an estimable wife by his side and an uninteresting family. The number of cashiers in Paris must always be a problem for the physiologist. Has any one as yet been able to state correctly the terms of the proportion sum wherein the cashier figures as the unknown x? Where will you find the man who shall live with wealth, like a cat with a caged mouse? This man, for further qualification, shall be capable of sitting boxed in behind an iron grating for seven or eight hours a day during seven-eighths of the year, perched upon a cane-seated chair in a space as narrow as a lieutenant's cabin on board a man-of-war. Such a man must be able to defy anchylosis of the knee and thigh joints; he must have a soul above meanness, in order to live meanly; must lose all relish for money by dint of handling it. Demand this peculiar specimen of any creed, educational system, school, or institution you please, and select Paris, that city of fiery ordeals and branch establishment of hell, as the soil in which to plant the said cashier. So be it. Creeds, schools, institutions and moral systems, all human rules and regulations, great and small, will, one after another, present much the same face that an intimate friend turns upon you when you ask him to lend you a thousand francs. With a dolorous dropping of the jaw, they indicate the guillotine, much as your friend aforesaid will furnish you with the address of the money-lender, pointing you to one of the hundred gates by which a man comes to the last refuge of the destitute.

Yet nature has her freaks in the making of a man's mind; she indulges herself and makes a few honest folk now and again, and now and then a cashier.

Melmoth Reconciled

Wherefore, that race of corsairs whom we dignify with the title of bankers, the gentry who take out a license for which they pay a thousand crowns, as the privateer takes out his letters of marque, hold these rare products of the incubations of virtue in such esteem that they confine them in cages in their counting-houses, much as governments procure and maintain specimens of strange beasts at their own charges.

If the cashier is possessed of an imagination or of a fervid temperament; if, as will sometimes happen to the most complete cashier, he loves his wife, and that wife grows tired of her lot, has ambitions, or merely some vanity in her composition, the cashier is undone. Search the chronicles of the counting-house. You will not find a single instance of a cashier attaining *a position*, as it is called. They are sent to the hulks; they go to foreign parts; they vegetate on a second floor in the Rue Saint-Louis among the market gardens of the Marais. Some day, when the cashiers of Paris come to a sense of their real value, a cashier will be hardly obtainable for money. Still, certain it is that there are people who are fit for nothing but to be cashiers, just as the bent of a certain order of mind inevitably makes for rascality. But, oh marvel of our civilization! Society rewards virtue with an income of a hundred louis in old age, a dwelling on a second floor, bread sufficient, occasional new bandana handkerchiefs, an elderly wife and her offspring.

So much for virtue. But for the opposite course, a little boldness, a faculty for keeping on the windward side of the law, as Turenne outflanked Montecuculi, and Society will sanction the theft of millions, shower ribbons upon the thief, cram him with honors, and smother him with consideration.

Government, moreover, works harmoniously with this profoundly illogical reasoner—Society. Government levies a conscription on the young intelligence of the kingdom at the age of seventeen or eighteen, a conscription of precocious brain-work before it is sent up to be submitted to a process of selection. Nurserymen sort and select seeds in much the same way. To this process the Government brings professional appraisers of talent, men who can assay brains as experts assay gold at the Mint. Five hundred such heads, set afire with hope, are sent up annually by the most progressive portion of the population; and of these the Government takes one-third, puts them in sacks called the Ecoles, and shakes them up together for three years. Though every one of these young plants represents vast productive power, they are made, as one may say, into cashiers. They receive appointments; the rank and file of engineers is made up of them; they are employed as captains of artillery; there is no (subaltern) grade to which they may not aspire. Finally, when these men, the pick of the youth of the nation, fattened on mathematics and stuffed with knowledge, have attained the age of fifty years, they have their reward, and receive as the price of their services the third-floor lodging, the wife and family, and all the comforts that sweeten life for mediocrity. If from among this race of dupes there should escape some five or six men of genius who climb the highest heights, is it not miraculous?

This is an exact statement of the relations between Talent and Probity on the one hand and Government and Society on the other, in an age that considers itself to be progressive. Without this prefatory explanation a recent occurrence in Paris would seem improbable; but preceded by this summing up of the situation, it will perhaps receive some thoughtful attention from minds capable of recognizing the real plague-spots of our civilization, a civilization which since 1815 as been moved by the spirit of gain rather than by principles of honor.

About five o'clock, on a dull autumn afternoon, the cashier of one of the largest banks in Paris was still at his desk, working by the light of a lamp that had been lit for some time. In accordance with the use and wont of commerce, the counting-house was in the darkest corner of the low-ceiled and far from spacious mezzanine floor, and at the very end of a passage lighted only by borrowed lights. The office doors along this corridor, each with its label, gave the place the look of a bath-house. At four o'clock the stolid porter had proclaimed, according to his orders, "The bank is closed." And by this time the departments were deserted, wives of the partners in the firm were expecting their lovers; the two bankers dining with their mistresses. Everything was in order.

The place where the strong boxes had been bedded in sheet-iron was just behind the little sanctum, where the cashier was busy. Doubtless he was balancing his books. The open front gave a glimpse of a safe of hammered iron, so enormously heavy (thanks to the science of the modern inventor) that burglars could not carry it away. The door only opened at the pleasure of those who knew its password. The letter-lock was a warden who kept its own secret and could not be bribed; the mysterious word was an ingenious realization of the "Open sesame!" in the *Arabian Nights*. But even this was as nothing. A man might discover the password; but unless he knew the lock's final secret, the *ultima ratio* of this gold-guarding dragon of mechanical science, it discharged a blunderbuss at his head.

The door of the room, the walls of the room, the shutters of the windows in the room, the whole place, in fact, was lined with sheet-iron a third of an inch in thickness, concealed behind the thin wooden paneling. The shutters had been closed, the door had been shut. If ever man could feel confident that he was absolutely alone, and that there was no remote possibility of being watched by prying eyes, that man was the cashier of the house of Nucingen and Company, in the Rue Saint-Lazare.

Accordingly the deepest silence prevailed in that iron cave. The fire had died out in the stove, but the room was full of that tepid warmth which produces the dull heavy-headedness and nauseous queasiness of a morning after an orgy. The stove is a mesmerist that plays no small part in the reduction of bank clerks and porters to a state of idiocy.

A room with a stove in it is a retort in which the power of strong men is evaporated, where their vitality is exhausted, and their wills enfeebled. Government offices are part of a great scheme for the manufacture of the mediocrity necessary for the maintenance of a Feudal System on a pecuniary basis—and money is the foundation of the Social Contract. (See *Les Employes*.) The mephitic vapors in the atmosphere of a crowded room contribute in no small degree to bring about a gradual deterioration of intelligences, the brain that gives off the largest quantity of nitrogen asphyxiates the others, in the long run.

The cashier was a man of five-and-forty or thereabouts. As he sat at the table, the light from a moderator lamp shining full on his bald head and glistening fringe of iron-gray hair that surrounded it—this baldness and the round outlines of his face made his head look very like a ball. His complexion was brick-red, a few wrinkles had gathered about his eyes, but he had the smooth, plump hands of a stout man. His blue cloth coat, a little rubbed and worn, and the creases and shininess of his trousers, traces of hard wear that the clothes-brush fails to remove, would impress a superficial observer with the idea that here was a thrifty and upright human being, sufficient of the philosopher or of the aristocrat to wear shabby clothes. But, unluckily, it is easy to find penny-wise people who will prove weak, wasteful, or incompetent in the capital things of life.

The cashier wore the ribbon of the Legion of Honor at his button-hole, for he had been a major of dragoons in the time of the Emperor. M. de Nucingen, who had been a contractor before he became a banker, had had reason in those days to know the honorable disposition of his cashier, who then occupied a high position. Reverses of fortune had befallen the major, and the banker out of regard for him paid him five hundred francs a month. The soldier had become a cashier in the year 1813, after his recovery from a wound received at Studzianka during the Retreat from Moscow, followed by six months of enforced idleness at Strasbourg, whither several officers had been transported by order of the Emperor, that they might receive skilled attention. This particular officer, Castanier by name, retired with the honorary grade of colonel, and a pension of two thousand four hundred francs.

In ten years' time the cashier had completely effaced the soldier, and Castanier inspired the banker with such trust in him, that he was associated in the transactions that went on in the private office behind his little counting-house. The baron himself had access to it by means of a secret staircase. There, matters of business were decided. It was the bolting-room where proposals were sifted; the privy council chamber where the reports of the money market were analyzed; circular notes issued thence; and finally, the private ledger and the journal which summarized the work of all the departments were kept there.

Castanier had gone himself to shut the door which opened on to a staircase that led to the parlor occupied by the two bankers on the first floor of their hotel. This done, he had sat down at his desk again, and for a moment he gazed at a little collection of letters of credit drawn on the firm of Watschildine of London. Then he had taken up the pen and imitated the banker's signature on each. *Nucingen* he wrote, and eyed the forged signatures critically to see which seemed the most perfect copy.

Suddenly he looked up as if a needle had pricked him. "You are not alone!" a boding voice seemed to cry in his heart; and indeed the forger saw a man standing at the little grated window of the counting-house, a man whose breathing was so noiseless that he did not seem to breathe at all. Castanier looked, and saw that the door at the end of the passage was wide open; the stranger must have entered by that way.

For the first time in his life the old soldier felt a sensation of dread that made him stare open-mouthed and wide-eyed at the man before him; and for that matter, the appearance of the apparition was sufficiently alarming even if unaccompanied by the mysterious circumstances of so sudden an entry. The rounded forehead, the harsh coloring of the long oval face, indicated quite as plainly as the cut of his clothes that the man was an Englishman, reeking of his native isles. You had only to look at the collar of his overcoat, at the voluminous cravat which smothered the crushed frills of a shirt front so white that it brought out the changeless leaden hue of an impassive face, and the thin red line of the lips that seemed made to suck the blood of corpses; and you can guess at once at the black gaiters buttoned up to the knee, and the half-puritanical costume of a wealthy Englishman dressed for a walking excursion. The intolerable glitter of the stranger's eyes produced a vivid and unpleasant impression, which was only deepened by the rigid outlines of his features. The dried-up, emaciated creature seemed to carry within him some gnawing thought that consumed him and could not be appeased.

He must have digested his food so rapidly that he could doubtless eat continually without bringing any trace of color into his face or features. A tun of Tokay *vin de succession* would not have caused any faltering in that piercing glance that read men's inmost thoughts, nor dethroned the merciless reasoning faculty that always seemed to go to the bottom of things. There was something of the fell and tranquil majesty of a tiger about him.

"I have come to cash this bill of exchange, sir," he said. Castanier felt the tones of his voice thrill through every nerve with a violent shock similar to that given by a discharge of electricity.

"The safe is closed," said Castanier.

"It is open," said the Englishman, looking round the counting-house. "To-morrow is Sunday, and I cannot wait. The amount is for five hundred thousand francs. You have the money there, and I must have it."

"But how did you come in, sir?"

The Englishman smiled. That smile frightened Castanier. No words could have replied more fully nor more peremptorily than that scornful and imperial curl of the stranger's lips. Castanier turned away, took up fifty packets each containing ten thousand francs in bank-notes, and held them out to the stranger, receiving in exchange for them a bill accepted by the Baron de Nucingen. A sort of convulsive tremor ran through him as he saw a red gleam in the stranger's eyes when they fell on the forged signature on the letter of credit.

"It... it wants your signature..." stammered Castanier, handing back the bill.

"Hand me your pen," answered the Englishman.

Castanier handed him the pen with which he had just committed forgery. The stranger wrote *John Melmoth*, then he returned the slip of paper and the pen to the cashier. Castanier looked at the handwriting, noticing that it sloped from right to left in the Eastern fashion, and Melmoth disappeared so noiselessly that when Castanier looked up again an exclamation broke from him, partly because the man was no longer there, partly because he felt a strange painful sensation such as our imagination might take for an effect of poison.

The pen that Melmoth had handled sent the same sickening heat through him that an emetic produces. But it seemed impossible to

Castanier that the Englishman should have guessed his crime. His inward qualms he attributed to the palpitation of the heart that, according to received ideas, was sure to follow at once on such a "turn" as the stranger had given him.

"The devil take it; I am very stupid. Providence is watching over me; for if that brute had come round to see my gentleman to-morrow, my goose would have been cooked!" said Castanier, and he burned the unsuccessful attempts at forgery in the stove.

He put the bill that he meant to take with him in an envelope, and helped himself to five hundred thousand francs in French and English bank-notes from the safe, which he locked. Then he put everything in order, lit a candle, blew out the lamp, took up his hat and umbrella, and went out sedately, as usual, to leave one of the two keys of the strong room with Madame de Nucingen, in the absence of her husband the Baron.

"You are in luck, M. Castanier," said the banker's wife as he entered the room; "we have a holiday on Monday; you can go into the country, or to Soizy."

"Madame, will you be so good as to tell your husband that the bill of exchange on Watschildine, which was behind time, has just been presented? The five hundred thousand francs have been paid; so I shall not come back till noon on Tuesday."

"Good-bye, monsieur; I hope you will have a pleasant time."

"The same to you, madame," replied the old dragoon as he went out. He glanced as he spoke at a young man well known in fashionable society at that time, a M. de Rastignac, who was regarded as Madame de Nucingen's lover.

"Madame," remarked this latter, "the old boy looks to me as if he meant to play you some ill turn."

"Pshaw! impossible; he is too stupid."

"Piquoizeau," said the cashier, walking into the porter's room, "what made you let anybody come up after four o'clock?"

"I have been smoking a pipe here in the doorway ever since four o'clock," said the man, "and nobody has gone into the bank. Nobody has come out either except the gentlemen——"

"Are you quite sure?"

"Yes, upon my word and honor. Stay, though, at four o'clock M. Werbrust's friend came, a young fellow from Messrs. du Tillet & Co., in the Rue Joubert."

"All right," said Castanier, and he hurried away.

The sickening sensation of heat that he had felt when he took back the pen returned in greater intensity. "*Mille diables!*" thought he, as he threaded his way along the Boulevard de Gand, "haven't I taken proper precautions? Let me think! Two clear days, Sunday and Monday, then a day of uncertainty before they begin to look for me; altogether, three days and four nights' respite. I have a couple of passports and two different disguises; is not that enough to throw the cleverest detective off the scent? On Tuesday morning I shall draw a million francs in London before the slightest suspicion has been aroused. My debts I am leaving behind for the benefit of my creditors, who will put a 'P' * on the bills, and I shall live comfortably in Italy for the rest of my days as the Conte Ferraro. [*Protested.] I was alone with him when he died, poor fellow, in the marsh of Zembin, and I shall slip into his skin.... *Mille diables!* the woman who is to follow after me might give them a clue! Think of an old campaigner like me infatuated enough to tie myself to a petticoat tail!... Why take her? I must leave her behind. Yes, I could make up my mind to it; but—I know myself—I should be ass enough to go back to her. Still, nobody knows Aquilina. Shall I take her or leave her?"

"You will not take her!" cried a voice that filled Castanier with sickening dread. He turned sharply, and saw the Englishman.

"The devil is in it!" cried the cashier aloud.

Melmoth had passed his victim by this time; and if Castanier's first impulse had been to fasten a quarrel on a man who read his own thoughts, he was so much torn up by opposing feelings that the immediate result was a temporary paralysis. When he resumed his walk he fell once more into that fever of irresolution which besets those who are so carried away by passion that they are ready to commit a crime, but have not sufficient strength of character to keep it to themselves without suffering terribly in the process. So, although Castanier had made up his mind to reap the fruits of a crime which was already half executed, he hesitated to carry out his designs. For him, as for many men of mixed character in whom weakness and strength are equally blended, the least trifling consideration determines whether they shall continue to lead blameless lives or become actively criminal. In the vast masses of men enrolled in Napoleon's armies there are many who, like Castanier, possessed the purely physical courage demanded on the battlefield, yet lacked the moral courage which makes a man as great in crime as he could have been in virtue.

The letter of credit was drafted in such terms that immediately on his arrival he might draw twenty-five thousand pounds on the firm of Watschildine, the London correspondents of the house of Nucingen. The London house had already been advised of the draft about to be made upon them, he had written to them himself. He had instructed an agent (chosen at random) to take his passage in a vessel which was to leave Portsmouth with a wealthy English family on board, who were going to Italy, and the passage-money had been paid in the name of the Conte Ferraro. The smallest details of the scheme had been thought out. He had arranged matters so as to divert the search that would be made for him into Belgium and Switzerland, while he himself was at sea in the English vessel. Then, by the time that Nucingen might flatter himself that he was on the track of his late cashier, the said cashier, as the Conte Ferraro, hoped to be safe in Naples. He had determined to disfigure his face in order to disguise himself the more completely, and by means of an acid to imitate the scars of smallpox. Yet, in spite of all these precautions, which surely seemed as if they must secure him complete immunity, his conscience tormented him; he was afraid. The even and peaceful life that he had led for so long had modified the morality of the camp. His life was stainless as yet; he could not sully it without a pang. So for the last time he abandoned himself to all the influences of the better self that strenuously resisted.

Melmoth Reconciled

"Pshaw!" he said at last, at the corner of the Boulevard and the Rue Montmartre, "I will take a cab after the play this evening and go out to Versailles. A post-chaise will be ready for me at my old quartermaster's place. He would keep my secret even if a dozen men were standing ready to shoot him down. The chances are all in my favor, so far as I see; so I shall take my little Naqui with me, and I will go."

"You will not go!" exclaimed the Englishman, and the strange tones of his voice drove all the cashier's blood back to his heart.

Melmoth stepped into a tilbury which was waiting for him, and was whirled away so quickly, that when Castanier looked up he saw his foe some hundred paces away from him, and before it even crossed his mind to cut off the man's retreat the tilbury was far on its way up the Boulevard Montmartre.

"Well, upon my word, there is something supernatural about this!" said he to himself. "If I were fool enough to believe in God, I should think that He had set Saint Michael on my tracks. Suppose that the devil and the police should let me go on as I please, so as to nab me in the nick of time? Did any one ever see the like! But there, this is folly..."

Castanier went along the Rue du Faubourg-Montmartre, slackening his pace as he neared the Rue Richer. There on the second floor of a block of buildings which looked out upon some gardens lived the unconscious cause of Castanier's crime—a young woman known in the quarter as Mme. de la Garde. A concise history of certain events in the cashier's past life must be given in order to explain these facts, and to give a complete presentment of the crisis when he yielded to temptation.

Mme. de la Garde said that she was a Piedmontese. No one, not even Castanier, knew her real name. She was one of those young girls, who are driven by dire misery, by inability to earn a living, or by fear of starvation, to have recourse to a trade which most of them loathe, many regard with indifference, and some few follow in obedience to the laws of their constitution. But on the brink of the gulf of prostitution in Paris, the young girl of sixteen, beautiful and pure as the Madonna, had met with Castanier. The old dragoon was too rough and homely to make his way in society, and he was tired of tramping the boulevard at night and of the kind of conquests made there by gold. For some time past he had desired to bring a certain regularity into an irregular life. He was struck by the beauty of the poor child who had drifted by chance into his arms, and his determination to rescue her from the life of the streets was half benevolent, half selfish, as some of the thoughts of the best of men are apt to be. Social conditions mingle elements of evil with the promptings of natural goodness of heart, and the mixture of motives underlying a man's intentions should be leniently judged. Castanier had just cleverness enough to be very shrewd where his own interests were concerned. So he concluded to be a philanthropist on either count, and at first made her his mistress.

"Hey! hey!" he said to himself, in his soldierly fashion. "I am an old wolf, and a sheep shall not make a fool of me. Castanier, old man, before you set up housekeeping, reconnoitre the girl's character for a bit, and see if she is a steady sort."

This irregular union gave the Piedmontese a status the most nearly approaching respectability among those which the world declines to recognize. During the first year she took the *nom de guerre* of Aquilina, one of the characters in *Venice Preserved* which she had chanced to read. She fancied that she resembled the courtesan in face and general appearance, and in a certain precocity of heart and brain of which she was conscious. When Castanier found that her life was as well regulated and virtuous as was possible for a social outlaw, he manifested a desire that they should live as husband and wife. So she took the name of Mme. de la Garde, in order to approach, as closely as Parisian usages permit, the conditions of a real marriage. As a matter of fact, many of these unfortunate girls have one fixed idea, to be looked upon as respectable middle-class women, who lead humdrum lives of faithfulness to their husbands; women who would make excellent mothers, keepers of household accounts, and menders of household linen. This longing springs from a sentiment so laudable, that society should take it into consideration. But society, incorrigible as ever, will assuredly persist in regarding the married woman as a corvette duly authorized by her flag and papers to go on her own course, while the woman who is a wife in all but name is a pirate and an outlaw for lack of a document. A day came when Mme. de la Garde would fain have signed herself "Mme. Castanier." The cashier was put out by this.

"So you do not love me well enough to marry me?" she said.

Castanier did not answer; he was absorbed by his thoughts. The poor girl resigned herself to her fate. The ex-dragoon was in despair. Naqui's heart softened towards him at the sight of his trouble; she tried to soothe him, but what could she do when she did not know what ailed him? When Naqui made up her mind to know the secret, although she never asked him a question, the cashier dolefully confessed to the existence of a Mme. Castanier. This lawful wife, a thousand times accursed, was living in a humble way in Strasbourg on a small property there; he wrote to her twice a year, and kept the secret of her existence so well, that no one suspected that he was married. The reason of this reticence? If it is familiar to many military men who may chance to be in a like predicament, it is perhaps worth while to give the story.

Your genuine trooper (if it is allowable here to employ the word which in the army signifies a man who is destined to die as a captain) is a sort of serf, a part and parcel of his regiment, an essentially simple creature, and Castanier was marked out by nature as a victim to the wiles of mothers with grown-up daughters left too long on their hands. It was at Nancy, during one of those brief intervals of repose when the Imperial armies were not on active service abroad, that Castanier was so unlucky as to pay some attention to a young lady with whom he danced at a *ridotto*, the provincial name for the entertainments often given by the military to the townsfolk, or vice versa, in garrison towns. A scheme for inveigling the gallant captain into matrimony was immediately set on foot, one of those schemes by which mothers secure accomplices in a human heart by touching all its motive springs, while they convert all their friends into fellow-conspirators. Like all people possessed by one idea, these ladies press everything into the service of their great project, slowly elaborating their toils, much as the ant-lion excavates its funnel in the sand and lies in wait at the bottom for its victim. Suppose that no one strays, after all, into that carefully constructed labyrinth? Suppose that the ant-lion dies of hunger and thirst in her pit? Such things may be, but if any heedless creature once enters in, it never comes out. All the wires which could be pulled to induce action on the captain's part were tried; appeals were made to the secret interested motives that always come into play in such cases; they worked on Castanier's hopes and on the weaknesses and vanity of human nature. Unluckily, he had praised the daughter to her mother when he brought her back after a waltz, a little chat followed, and then an invitation in the most natural way in the world. Once introduced into the house, the dragoon was dazzled by the hospitality of a family who appeared to conceal their real wealth beneath a show of careful economy. He was skilfully flattered on all sides, and every one extolled for his benefit the various treasures there displayed. A neatly timed dinner, served on plate lent by an uncle, the attention shown to him by the only daughter of the house, the gossip of the town, a well-to-do sub-lieutenant who seemed likely to cut the ground from under his feet—all the innumerable snares, in short, of the provincial ant-lion were set for him, and to such good purpose, that Castanier said five years later, "To this day I do not know how it came about!"

The dragoon received fifteen thousand francs with the lady, who after two years of marriage, became the ugliest and consequently the most peevish woman on earth. Luckily they had no children. The fair complexion (maintained by a Spartan regimen), the fresh, bright color in her face, which spoke of an engaging modesty, became overspread with blotches and pimples; her figure, which had seemed so straight, grew crooked, the angel became a suspicious and shrewish creature who drove Castanier frantic. Then the fortune took to itself wings. At length the dragoon, no longer recognizing the woman whom he had wedded, left her to live on a little property at Strasbourg, until the time when it should please God to remove her to adorn Paradise. She was one of those virtuous women who, for want of other occupation, would weary the life out of an angel with complainings, who pray till (if their prayers are heard in heaven) they must exhaust the patience of the Almighty, and say everything that is bad of their husbands in dovelike murmurs over a game of boston with their neighbors. When Aquilina learned all these troubles she clung still more affectionately to Castanier, and made him so happy, varying with woman's ingenuity the pleasures with which she filled his life, that all unwittingly she was the cause of the cashier's downfall.

Like many women who seem by nature destined to sound all the depths of love, Mme. de la Garde was disinterested. She asked neither for gold nor for jewelry, gave no thought to the future, lived entirely for the present and for the pleasures of the present. She accepted expensive ornaments and dresses, the carriage so eagerly coveted by women of her class, as one harmony the more in the picture of life. There was absolutely no vanity in her desire not to appear at a better advantage but to look the fairer, and moreover, no woman could live without luxuries more cheerfully. When a man of generous nature (and military men are mostly of this stamp) meets with such a woman, he feels a sort of exasperation at finding himself her debtor in generosity. He feels that he could stop a mail coach to obtain money for her if he has not sufficient for her whims. He will commit a crime if so he may be great and noble in the eyes of some woman or of his special public; such is the nature of the man. Such a lover is like a gambler who would be dishonored in his own eyes if he did not repay the sum he borrowed from a waiter in a gaming-house; but will shrink from no crime, will leave his wife and children without a penny, and rob and murder, if so he may come to the gaming-table with a full purse, and his honor remain untarnished among the frequenters of that fatal abode. So it was with Castanier.

He had begun by installing Aquiline is a modest fourth-floor dwelling, the furniture being of the simplest kind. But when he saw the girl's beauty and great qualities, when he had known inexpressible and unlooked-for happiness with her, he began to dote upon her; and longed to adorn his idol. Then Aquilina's toilette was so comically out of keeping with her poor abode, that for both their sakes it was clearly incumbent on him to move. The change swallowed up almost all Castanier's savings, for he furnished his domestic paradise with all the prodigality that is lavished on a kept mistress. A pretty woman must have everything pretty about her; the unity of charm in the woman and her surroundings singles her out from among her sex. This sentiment of homogeneity indeed, though it has frequently escaped the attention of observers, is instinctive in human nature; and the same prompting leads elderly spinsters to surround themselves with dreary relics of the past. But the lovely Piedmontese must have the newest and latest fashions, and all that was daintiest and prettiest in stuffs for hangings, in silks or jewelry, in fine china and other brittle and fragile wares. She asked for nothing; but when she was called upon to make a choice, when Castanier asked her, "Which do you like?" she would answer, "Why, this is the nicest!" Love never counts the cost, and Castanier therefore always took the "nicest."

When once the standard had been set up, there was nothing for it but everything in the household must be in conformity, from the linen, plate, and crystal through a thousand and one items of expenditure down to the pots and pans in the kitchen. Castanier had meant to "do things simply," as the saying goes, but he gradually found himself more and more in debt. One expense entailed another. The clock called for candle sconces. Fires must be lighted in the ornamental grates, but the curtains and hangings were too fresh and delicate to be soiled by smuts, so they must be replaced by patent and elaborate fireplaces, warranted to give out no smoke, recent inventions of the people who are so clever at drawing up a prospectus. Then Aquilina found it so nice to run about barefooted on the carpet in her room, that Castanier must have soft carpets laid everywhere for the pleasure of playing with Naqui. A bathroom, too, was built for her, everything to the end that she might be more comfortable.

Shopkeepers, workmen, and manufacturers in Paris have a mysterious knack of enlarging a hole in a man's purse. They cannot give the price of anything upon inquiry; and as the paroxysm of longing cannot abide delay, orders are given by the feeble light of an approximate estimate of cost. The same people never send in the bills at once, but ply the purchaser with furniture till his head spins. Everything is so pretty, so charming; and every one is satisfied.

A few months later the obliging furniture dealers are metamorphosed, and reappear in the shape of alarming totals on invoices that fill the soul with their horrid clamor; they are in urgent want of the money; they are, as you may say on the brink of bankruptcy, their tears flow, it is heartrending to hear them! And then——the gulf yawns, and gives up serried columns of figures marching four deep, when as a matter of fact they should have issued innocently three by three.

Before Castanier had any idea of how much he had spent, he had arranged for Aquilina to have a carriage from a livery stable when she went out, instead of a cab. Castanier was a gourmand; he engaged an excellent cook; and Aquilina, to please him, had herself made the purchases of early fruit and vegetables, rare delicacies, and exquisite wines. But, as Aquilina had nothing of her own, these gifts of hers, so precious by reason of the thought and tact and graciousness that prompted them, were no less a drain upon Castanier's purse; he did not like his Naqui to be without money, and Naqui could not keep money in her pocket. So the table was a heavy item of expenditure for a man with Castanier's income. The ex-dragoon was compelled to resort to various shifts for obtaining money, for he could not bring himself to renounce this delightful life. He loved the woman too well to cross the freaks of the mistress. He was one of those men who, through self-love or through weakness of character, can refuse nothing to a woman; false shame overpowers them, and they rather face ruin than make the admissions: "I cannot——" "My means will not permit——" "I cannot afford——"

When, therefore, Castanier saw that if he meant to emerge from the abyss of debt into which he had plunged, he must part with Aquilina and live upon bread and water, he was so unable to do without her or to change his habits of life, that daily he put off his plans of reform until the morrow. The debts were pressing, and he began by borrowing money. His position and previous character inspired confidence, and of this he took advantage to devise a system of borrowing money as he required it. Then, as the total amount of debt rapidly increased, he had recourse to those commercial inventions known as accommodation bills. This form of bill does not represent goods or other value received, and the first endorser pays the amount named for the obliging person who accepts it. This species of fraud is tolerated because it is impossible to detect it, and, moreover, it is an imaginary fraud which only becomes real if payment is ultimately refused.

When at length it was evidently impossible to borrow any longer, whether because the amount of the debt was now so greatly increased, or because Castanier was unable to pay the large amount of interest on the aforesaid sums of money, the cashier saw bankruptcy before him. On making this discovery, he decided for a fraudulent bankruptcy rather than an ordinary failure, and preferred a crime to a misdemeanor. He determined, after the fashion of the celebrated cashier of the Royal Treasury, to abuse the trust deservedly won, and to increase the number of his creditors by making a final loan of the sum sufficient to keep him in comfort in a foreign country for the rest of his days. All this, as has been seen, he had prepared to do.

Aquilina knew nothing of the irksome cares of this life; she enjoyed her existence, as many a woman does, making no inquiry as to where the money came from, even as sundry other folk will eat their buttered rolls untroubled by any restless spirit of curiosity as to the culture and growth of wheat; but as the labor and miscalculations of agriculture lie on the other side of the baker's oven, so beneath the unappreciated luxury of many a Parisian household lie intolerable anxieties and exorbitant toil.

While Castanier was enduring the torture of the strain, and his thoughts were full of the deed that should change his whole life, Aquilina was lying luxuriously back in a great armchair by the fireside, beguiling the time by chatting with her waiting-maid. As frequently happens in such cases the maid had become the mistress' confidant, Jenny having first assured herself that her mistress' ascendency over Castanier was complete.

"What are we to do this evening? Leon seems determined to come," Mme. de la Garde was saying, as she read a passionate epistle indited upon a faint gray notepaper.

"Here is the master!" said Jenny.

Castanier came in. Aquilina, nowise disconcerted, crumpled up the letter, took it with the tongs, and held it in the flames.

"So that is what you do with your love-letters, is it?" asked Castanier.

"Oh goodness, yes," said Aquilina; "is it not the best way of keeping them safe? Besides, fire should go to fire, as water makes for the river."

"You are talking as if it were a real love-letter, Naqui— —"

"Well, am I not handsome enough to receive them?" she said, holding up her forehead for a kiss. There was a carelessness in her manner that would have told any man less blind than Castanier that it was only a piece of conjugal duty, as it were, to give this joy to the cashier, but use and wont had brought Castanier to the point where clear-sightedness is no longer possible for love.

"I have taken a box at the Gymnase this evening," he said; "let us have dinner early, and then we need not dine in a hurry."

"Go and take Jenny. I am tired of plays. I do not know what is the matter with me this evening; I would rather stay here by the fire."

"Come, all the same though, Naqui; I shall not be here to bore you much longer. Yes, Quiqui, I am going to start to-night, and it will be some time before I come back again. I am leaving everything in your charge. Will you keep your heart for me too?"

"Neither my heart nor anything else," she said; "but when you come back again, Naqui will still be Naqui for you."

"Well, this is frankness. So you would not follow me?"

"No."

"Why not?"

"Eh! why, how can I leave the lover who writes me such sweet little notes?" she asked, pointing to the blackened scrap of paper with a mocking smile.

"Is there any truth in it?" asked Castanier. "Have you really a lover?"

"Really!" cried Aquilina; "and have you never given it a serious thought, dear? To begin with, you are fifty years old. Then you have just the sort of face to put on a fruit stall; if the woman tried to see you for a pumpkin, no one would contradict her. You puff and blow like a seal when you come upstairs; your paunch rises and falls like a diamond on a woman's forehead! It is pretty plain that you served in the dragoons; you are a very ugly-looking old man. Fiddle-de-dee. If you have any mind to keep my respect, I recommend you not to add imbecility to these qualities by imagining that such a girl as I am will be content with your asthmatic love, and not look for youth and good looks and pleasure by way of a variety——"

"Aquilina! you are laughing, of course?"

"Oh, very well; and are you not laughing too? Do you take me for a fool, telling me that you are going away? 'I am going to start to-night!'" she said, mimicking his tones. "Stuff and nonsense! Would you talk like that if you were really going from your Naqui? You would cry, like the booby that you are!"

"After all, if I go, will you follow?" he asked.

"Tell me first whether this journey of yours is a bad joke or not."

"Yes, seriously, I am going."

"Well, then, seriously, I shall stay. A pleasant journey to you, my boy! I will wait till you come back. I would sooner take leave of life than take leave of my dear, cozy Paris——"

"Will you not come to Italy, to Naples, and lead a pleasant life there—a delicious, luxurious life, with this stout old fogy of yours, who puffs and blows like a seal?"

"No."

"Ungrateful girl!"

"Ungrateful?" she cried, rising to her feet. "I might leave this house this moment and take nothing out of it but myself. I shall have given you all the treasures a young girl can give, and something that not every drop in your veins and mine can ever give me back. If, by any means whatever, by selling my hopes of eternity, for instance, I could recover my past self, body and soul (for I have, perhaps, redeemed my soul), and be pure as a lily for my lover, I would not hesitate a moment! What sort of devotion has rewarded mine? You have housed and fed me, just as you give a dog food and a kennel because he is a protection to the house, and he may take kicks when we are out of humor, and lick our hands as soon as we are pleased to call him. And which of us two will have been the more generous?"

"Oh! dear child, do you not see that I am joking?" returned Castanier. "I am going on a short journey; I shall not be away for very long. But come with me to the Gymnase; I shall start just before midnight, after I have had time to say good-bye to you."

"Poor pet! so you are really going, are you?" she said. She put her arms round his neck, and drew down his head against her bodice.

"You are smothering me!" cried Castanier, with his face buried in Aquilina's breast. That damsel turned to say in Jenny's ear, "Go to Leon, and tell him not to come till one o'clock. If you do not find him, and he comes here during the leave-taking, keep him in your room.—Well," she went on, setting free Castanier, and giving a tweak to the tip of his nose, "never mind, handsomest of seals that you are. I will go to the theatre with you this evening? But all in good time; let us have dinner! There is a nice little dinner for you—just what you like."

"It is very hard to part from such a woman as you!" exclaimed Castanier.

"Very well then, why do you go?" asked she.

"Ah! why? why? If I were to begin to begin to explain the reasons why, I must tell you things that would prove to you that I love you almost to madness. Ah! if you have sacrificed your honor for me, I have sold mine for you; we are quits. Is that love?"

"What is all this about?" said she. "Come, now, promise me that if I had a lover you would still love me as a father; that would be love! Come, now, promise it at once, and give us your fist upon it."

"I should kill you," and Castanier smiled as he spoke.

They sat down to the dinner table, and went thence to the Gymnase. When the first part of the performance was over, it occurred to Castanier to show himself to some of his acquaintances in the house, so as to turn away any suspicion of his departure. He left Mme. de la Garde in the corner box where she was seated, according to her modest wont, and went to walk up and down in the lobby. He had not gone many paces before he saw the Englishman, and with a sudden return of the sickening sensation of heat that once before had vibrated through him, and of the terror that he had felt already, he stood face to face with Melmoth.

"Forger!"

At the word, Castanier glanced round at the people who were moving about them. He fancied that he could see astonishment and curiosity in their eyes, and wishing to be rid of this Englishman at once, he raised his hand to strike him—and felt his arm paralyzed by some invisible power that sapped his strength and nailed him to the spot. He allowed the stranger to take him by the arm, and they walked together to the green-room like two friends.

"Who is strong enough to resist me?" said the Englishman, addressing him. "Do you not know that everything here on earth must obey me, that it is in my power to do everything? I read men's thoughts, I see the future, and I know the past. I am here, and I can be elsewhere also. Time and space and distance are nothing to me. The whole world is at my beck and call. I have the power of continual enjoyment and of giving joy. I can see through walls, discover hidden treasures, and fill my hands with them. Palaces arise at my nod, and my architect makes no mistakes. I can make all lands break forth into blossom, heap up their gold and precious stones, and surround myself with fair women and ever new faces; everything is yielded up to my will. I could gamble on the Stock Exchange, and my speculations would be infallible; but a man who can find the hoards that misers have hidden in the earth need not trouble himself about stocks. Feel the strength of the hand that grasps you; poor wretch, doomed to shame! Try to bend the arm of iron! try to soften the adamantine heart! Fly from me if you dare! You would hear my voice in the depths of the caves that lie under the Seine; you might hide in the Catacombs, but would you not see me there? My voice could be heard through the sound of thunder, my eyes shine as brightly as the sun, for I am the peer of Lucifer!"

Castanier heard the terrible words, and felt no protest nor contradiction within himself. He walked side by side with the Englishman, and had no power to leave him.

Melmoth Reconciled

"You are mine; you have just committed a crime. I have found at last the mate whom I have sought. Have you a mind to learn your destiny? Aha! you came here to see a play, and you shall see a play — nay, two. Come. Present me to Mme. de la Garde as one of your best friends. Am I not your last hope of escape?"

Castanier, followed by the stranger, returned to his box; and in accordance with the order he had just received, he hastened to introduce Melmoth to Mme. de la Garde. Aquilina seemed to be not in the least surprised. The Englishman declined to take a seat in front, and Castanier was once more beside his mistress; the man's slightest wish must be obeyed. The last piece was about to begin, for, at that time, small theatres gave only three pieces. One of the actors had made the Gymnase the fashion, and that evening Perlet (the actor in question) was to play in a vaudeville called *Le Comedien d'Etampes*, in which he filled four different parts.

When the curtain rose, the stranger stretched out his hand over the crowded house. Castanier's cry of terror died away, for the walls of his throat seemed glued together as Melmoth pointed to the stage, and the cashier knew that the play had been changed at the Englishman's desire.

He saw the strong-room at the bank; he saw the Baron de Nucingen in conference with a police-officer from the Prefecture, who was informing him of Castanier's conduct, explaining that the cashier had absconded with money taken from the safe, giving the history of the forged signature. The information was put in writing; the document signed and duly despatched to the Public Prosecutor.

"Are we in time, do you think?" asked Nucingen.

"Yes," said the agent of police; "he is at the Gymnase, and has no suspicion of anything."

Castanier fidgeted on his chair, and made as if he would leave the theatre, but Melmoth's hand lay on his shoulder, and he was obliged to sit and watch; the hideous power of the man produced an effect like that of nightmare, and he could not move a limb. Nay, the man himself was the nightmare; his presence weighed heavily on his victim like a poisoned atmosphere. When the wretched cashier turned to implore the Englishman's mercy, he met those blazing eyes that discharged electric currents, which pierced through him and transfixed him like darts of steel.

"What have I done to you?" he said, in his prostrate helplessness, and he breathed hard like a stag at the water's edge. "What do you want of me?"

"Look!" cried Melmoth.

Castanier looked at the stage. The scene had been changed. The play seemed to be over, and Castanier beheld himself stepping from the carriage with Aquilina; but as he entered the courtyard of the house on the Rue Richer, the scene again was suddenly changed, and he saw his own house. Jenny was chatting by the fire in her mistress' room with a subaltern officer of a line regiment then stationed at Paris.

"He is going, is he?" said the sergeant, who seemed to belong to a family in easy circumstances; "I can be happy at my ease! I love Aquilina too well to allow her to belong to that old toad! I, myself, am going to marry Mme. de la Garde!" cried the sergeant.

"Old toad!" Castanier murmured piteously.

"Here come the master and mistress; hide yourself! Stay, get in here Monsieur Leon," said Jenny. "The master won't stay here for very long."

Castanier watched the sergeant hide himself among Aquilina's gowns in her dressing-room. Almost immediately he himself appeared upon the scene, and took leave of his mistress, who made fun of him in "asides" to Jenny, while she uttered the sweetest and tenderest words in his ears. She wept with one side of her face, and laughed with the other. The audience called for an encore.

"Accursed creature!" cried Castanier from his box.

Aquilina was laughing till the tears came into her eyes.

"Goodness!" she cried, "how funny Perlet is as the Englishwoman!... Why don't you laugh? Every one else in the house is laughing. Laugh, dear!" she said to Castanier.

Melmoth Reconciled

Melmoth burst out laughing, and the unhappy cashier shuddered. The Englishman's laughter wrung his heart and tortured his brain; it was as if a surgeon had bored his skull with a red-hot iron.

"Laughing! are they laughing!" stammered Castanier.

He did not see the prim English lady whom Perlet was acting with such ludicrous effect, nor hear the English-French that had filled the house with roars of laughter; instead of all this, he beheld himself hurrying from the Rue Richer, hailing a cab on the Boulevard, bargaining with the man to take him to Versailles. Then once more the scene changed. He recognized the sorry inn at the corner of the Rue de l'Orangerie and the Rue des Recollets, which was kept by his old quartermaster. It was two o'clock in the morning, the most perfect stillness prevailed, no one was there to watch his movements. The post-horses were put into the carriage (it came from a house in the Avenue de Paris in which an Englishman lived, and had been ordered in the foreigner's name to avoid raising suspicion). Castanier saw that he had his bills and his passports, stepped into the carriage, and set out. But at the barrier he saw two gendarmes lying in wait for the carriage. A cry of horror burst from him but Melmoth gave him a glance, and again the sound died in his throat.

"Keep your eyes on the stage, and be quiet!" said the Englishman.

In another moment Castanier saw himself flung into prison at the Conciergerie; and in the fifth act of the drama, entitled *The Cashier*, he saw himself, in three months' time, condemned to twenty years of penal servitude. Again a cry broke from him. He was exposed upon the Place du Palais-de-Justice, and the executioner branded him with a red-hot iron. Then came the last scene of all; among some sixty convicts in the prison yard of the Bicetre, he was awaiting his turn to have the irons riveted on his limbs.

"Dear me! I cannot laugh any more!..." said Aquilina. "You are very solemn, dear boy; what can be the matter? The gentleman has gone."

"A word with you, Castanier," said Melmoth when the piece was at an end, and the attendant was fastening Mme. de la Garde's cloak.

The corridor was crowded, and escape impossible.

"Very well, what is it?"

Melmoth Reconciled

"No human power can hinder you from taking Aquilina home, and going next to Versailles, there to be arrested."

"How so?"

"Because you are in a hand that will never relax its grasp," returned the Englishman.

Castanier longed for the power to utter some word that should blot him out from among living men and hide him in the lowest depths of hell.

"Suppose that the Devil were to make a bid for your soul, would you not give it to him now in exchange for the power of God? One single word, and those five hundred thousand francs shall be back in the Baron de Nucingen's safe; then you can tear up the letter of credit, and all traces of your crime will be obliterated. Moreover, you would have gold in torrents. You hardly believe in anything perhaps? Well, if all this comes to pass, you will believe at least in the Devil."

"If it were only possible!" said Castanier joyfully.

"The man who can do it all gives you his word that it is possible," answered the Englishman.

Melmoth, Castanier, and Mme. de la Garde were standing out in the Boulevard when Melmoth raised his arm. A drizzling rain was falling, the streets were muddy, the air was close, there was thick darkness overhead; but in a moment, as the arm was outstretched, Paris was filled with sunlight; it was high noon on a bright July day. The trees were covered with leaves; a double stream of joyous holiday makers strolled beneath them. Sellers of liquorice water shouted their cool drinks. Splendid carriages rolled past along the streets. A cry of terror broke from the cashier, and at that cry rain and darkness once more settled down upon the Boulevard.

Mme. de la Garde had stepped into the carriage. "Do be quick, dear!" she cried; "either come in or stay out. Really you are as dull as ditch-water this evening——"

"What must I do?" Castanier asked of Melmoth.

"Would you like to take my place?" inquired the Englishman.

"Yes."

"Very well, then; I will be at your house in a few moments."

"By the by, Castanier, you are rather off your balance," Aquilina remarked. "There is some mischief brewing: you were quite melancholy and thoughtful all through the play. Do you want anything that I can give you, dear? Tell me."

"I am waiting till we are at home to know whether you love me."

"You need not wait till then," she said, throwing her arms round his neck. "There!" she said, as she embraced him, passionately to all appearance, and plied him with the coaxing caresses that are part of the business of such a life as hers, like stage action for an actress.

"Where is the music?" asked Castanier.

"What next? Only think of your hearing music now!"

"Heavenly music!" he went on. "The sounds seem to come from above."

"What? You have always refused to give me a box at the Italiens because you could not abide music, and are you turning music-mad at this time of day? Mad—that you are! The music is inside your own noddle, old addle-pate!" she went on, as she took his head in her hands and rocked it to and fro on her shoulder. "Tell me now, old man; isn't it the creaking of the wheels that sings in your ears?"

"Just listen, Naqui! If the angels make music for God Almighty, it must be such music as this that I am drinking in at every pore, rather than hearing. I do no know how to tell you about it; it is as sweet as honey-water!"

"Why, of course, they have music in heaven, for the angels in all the pictures have harps in their hands. He is mad, upon my word!" she said to herself, as she saw Castanier's attitude; he looked like an opium-eater in a blissful trance.

They reached the house. Castanier, absorbed by the thought of all that he had just heard and seen, knew not whether to believe it or not; he was like a drunken man, and utterly unable to think connectedly. He came to himself in Aquilina's room, whither he had been supported by the united efforts of his mistress, the porter, and Jenny; for he had fainted as he stepped from the carriage.

"*He* will be here directly! Oh, my friends, my friends," he cried, and he flung himself despairingly into the depths of a low chair beside the fire.

Jenny heard the bell as he spoke, and admitted the Englishman. She announced that "a gentleman had come who had made an appointment with the master," when Melmoth suddenly appeared, and deep silence followed. He looked at the porter — the porter went; he looked at Jenny — and Jenny went likewise.

"Madame," said Melmoth, turning to Aquilina, "with your permission, we will conclude a piece of urgent business."

He took Castanier's hand, and Castanier rose, and the two men went into the drawing-room. There was no light in the room, but Melmoth's eyes lit up the thickest darkness. The gaze of those strange eyes had left Aquilina like one spellbound; she was helpless, unable to take any thought for her lover; moreover, she believed him to be safe in Jenny's room, whereas their early return had taken the waiting-woman by surprise, and she had hidden the officer in the dressing-room. It had all happened exactly as in the drama that Melmoth had displayed for his victim. Presently the house-door was slammed violently, and Castanier reappeared.

"What ails you?" cried the horror-struck Aquilina.

There was a change in the cashier's appearance. A strange pallor overspread his once rubicund countenance; it wore the peculiarly sinister and stony look of the mysterious visitor. The sullen glare of his eyes was intolerable, the fierce light in them seemed to scorch. The man who had looked so good-humored and good-natured had suddenly grown tyrannical and proud. The courtesan thought that Castanier had grown thinner; there was a terrible majesty in his brow; it was as if a dragon breathed forth a malignant influence that weighed upon the others like a close, heavy atmosphere. For a moment Aquilina knew not what to do.

"What has passed between you and that diabolical-looking man in those few minutes?" she asked at length.

"I have sold my soul to him. I feel it; I am no longer the same. He has taken my *self*, and given me his soul in exchange."

"What?"

"You would not understand it at all.... Ah! he was right," Castanier went on, "the fiend was right! I see everything and know all things.—You have been deceiving me!"

Aquilina turned cold with terror. Castanier lighted a candle and went into the dressing-room. The unhappy girl followed him with dazed bewilderment, and great was her astonishment when Castanier drew the dresses that hung there aside and disclosed the sergeant.

"Come out, my boy," said the cashier; and, taking Leon by a button of his overcoat, he drew the officer into his room.

The Piedmontese, haggard and desperate, had flung herself into her easy-chair. Castanier seated himself on a sofa by the fire, and left Aquilina's lover in a standing position.

"You have been in the army," said Leon; "I am ready to give you satisfaction."

"You are a fool," said Castanier drily. "I have no occasion to fight. I could kill you by a look if I had any mind to do it. I will tell you what it is, youngster; why should I kill you? I can see a red line round your neck—the guillotine is waiting for you. Yes, you will end in the Place de Greve. You are the headsman's property! there is no escape for you. You belong to a vendita, of the Carbonari. You are plotting against the Government."

"You did not tell me that," cried the Piedmontese, turning to Leon.

"So you do not know that the Minister decided this morning to put down your Society?" the cashier continued. "The Procureur-General has a list of your names. You have been betrayed. They are busy drawing up the indictment at this moment."

"Then was it you who betrayed him?" cried Aquilina, and with a hoarse sound in her throat like the growl of a tigress she rose to her feet; she seemed as if she would tear Castanier in pieces.

"You know me too well to believe it," Castanier retorted. Aquilina was benumbed by his coolness.

"Then how do you know it?" she murmured.

"I did not know it until I went into the drawing-room; now I know it—now I see and know all things, and can do all things."

The sergeant was overcome with amazement.

"Very well then, save him, save him, dear!" cried the girl, flinging herself at Castanier's feet. "If nothing is impossible to you, save him! I will love you, I will adore you, I will be your slave and not your mistress. I will obey your wildest whims; you shall do as you will with me. Yes, yes, I will give you more than love; you shall have a daughter's devotion as well as... Rodolphe! why will you not understand! After all, however violent my passions may be, I shall be yours for ever! What should I say to persuade you? I will invent pleasures... I... Great heavens! one moment! whatever you shall ask of me—to fling myself from the window for instance—you will need to say but one word, 'Leon!' and I will plunge down into hell. I would bear any torture, any pain of body or soul, anything you might inflict upon me!"

Castanier heard her with indifference. For an answer, he indicated Leon to her with a fiendish laugh.

"The guillotine is waiting for him," he repeated.

"No, no, no! He shall not leave this house. I will save him!" she cried. "Yes; I will kill any one who lays a finger upon him! Why will you not save him?" she shrieked aloud; her eyes were blazing, her hair unbound. "Can you save him?"

"I can do everything."

"Why do you not save him?"

"Why?" shouted Castanier, and his voice made the ceiling ring.— "Eh! it is my revenge! Doing evil is my trade!"

"Die?" said Aquilina; "must he die, my lover? Is it possible?"

She sprang up and snatched a stiletto from a basket that stood on the chest of drawers and went to Castanier, who now began to laugh.

Melmoth Reconciled

"You know very well that steel cannot hurt me now——"

Aquilina's arm suddenly dropped like a snapped harp string.

"Out with you, my good friend," said the cashier, turning to the sergeant, "and go about your business."

He held out his hand; the other felt Castanier's superior power, and could not choose but to obey.

"This house is mine; I could send for the commissary of police if I chose, and give you up as a man who has hidden himself on my premises, but I would rather let you go; I am a fiend, I am not a spy."

"I shall follow him!" said Aquilina.

"Then follow him," returned Castanier.—"Here, Jenny——"

Jenny appeared.

"Tell the porter to hail a cab for them.—Here Naqui," said Castanier, drawing a bundle of bank-notes from his pocket; "you shall not go away like a pauper from a man who loves you still."

He held out three hundred thousand francs. Aquilina took the notes, flung them on the floor, spat on them, and trampled upon them in a frenzy of despair.

"We will leave this house on foot," she cried, "without a farthing of your money.—Jenny, stay where you are."

"Good-evening!" answered the cashier, as he gathered up the notes again. "I have come back from my journey.—Jenny," he added, looking at the bewildered waiting-maid, "you seem to me to be a good sort of girl. You have no mistress now. Come here. This evening you shall have a master."

Aquilina, who felt safe nowhere, went at once with the sergeant to the house of one of her friends. But all Leon's movements were suspiciously watched by the police, and after a time he and three of his friends were arrested. The whole story may be found in the newspapers of that day.

Castanier felt that he had undergone a mental as well as a physical transformation. The Castanier of old no longer existed—the boy, the young Lothario, the soldier who had proved his courage, who had been tricked into a marriage and disillusioned, the cashier, the passionate lover who had committed a crime for Aquilina's sake. His inmost nature had suddenly asserted itself. His brain had expanded, his senses had developed. His thoughts comprehended the whole world; he saw all the things of earth as if he had been raised to some high pinnacle above the world.

Until that evening at the play he had loved Aquilina to distraction. Rather than give her up he would have shut his eyes to her infidelities; and now all that blind passion had passed away as a cloud vanishes in the sunlight.

Jenny was delighted to succeed to her mistress' position and fortune, and did the cashier's will in all things; but Castanier, who could read the inmost thoughts of the soul, discovered the real motive underlying this purely physical devotion. He amused himself with her, however, like a mischievous child who greedily sucks the juice of the cherry and flings away the stone. The next morning at breakfast time, when she was fully convinced that she was a lady and the mistress of the house, Castanier uttered one by one the thoughts that filled her mind as she drank her coffee.

"Do you know what you are thinking, child?" he said, smiling. "I will tell you: 'So all that lovely rosewood furniture that I coveted so much, and the pretty dresses that I used to try on, are mine now! All on easy terms that Madame refused, I do no know why. My word! if I might drive about in a carriage, have jewels and pretty things, a box at the theatre, and put something by! with me he should lead a life of pleasure fit to kill him if he were not as strong as a Turk! I never saw such a man!'—Was not that just what you were thinking," he went on, and something in his voice made Jenny turn pale. "Well, yes, child; you could not stand it, and I am sending you away for your own good; you would perish in the attempt. Come, let us part good friends," and he coolly dismissed her with a very small sum of money.

The first use that Castanier had promised himself that he would make of the terrible power brought at the price of his eternal happiness, was the full and complete indulgence of all his tastes.

He first put his affairs in order, readily settled his accounts with M. de Nucingen, who found a worthy German to succeed him, and then determined on a carouse worthy of the palmiest days of the Roman Empire. He plunged into dissipation as recklessly as Belshazzar of old went to that last feast in Babylon. Like Belshazzar, he saw clearly through his revels a gleaming hand that traced his doom in letters of flame, not on the narrow walls of the banqueting-chamber, but over the vast spaces of heaven that the rainbow spans. His feast was not, indeed, an orgy confined within the limits of a banquet, for he squandered all the powers of soul and body in exhausting all the pleasures of earth. The table was in some sort earth itself, the earth that trembled beneath his feet. His was the last festival of the reckless spendthrift who has thrown all prudence to the winds. The devil had given him the key of the storehouse of human pleasures; he had filled and refilled his hands, and he was fast nearing the bottom. In a moment he had felt all that that enormous power could accomplish; in a moment he had exercised it, proved it, wearied of it. What had hitherto been the sum of human desires became as nothing. So often it happens that with possession the vast poetry of desire must end, and the thing possessed is seldom the thing that we dreamed of.

Beneath Melmoth's omnipotence lurked this tragical anticlimax of so many a passion, and now the inanity of human nature was revealed to his successor, to whom infinite power brought Nothingness as a dowry.

To come to a clear understanding of Castanier's strange position, it must be borne in mind how suddenly these revolutions of thought and feeling had been wrought; how quickly they had succeeded each other; and of these things it is hard to give any idea to those who have never broken the prison bonds of time, and space, and distance. His relation to the world without had been entirely changed with the expansion of his faculties.

Like Melmoth himself, Castanier could travel in a few moments over the fertile plains of India, could soar on the wings of demons above African desert spaces, or skim the surface of the seas. The same insight that could read the inmost thoughts of others, could apprehend at a glance the nature of any material object, just as he caught as it were all flavors at once upon his tongue. He took his pleasure like a despot; a blow of the axe felled the tree that he might eat its fruits. The transitions, the alternations that measure joy and pain, and diversify human happiness, no longer existed for him. He had so completely glutted his appetites that pleasure must overpass the limits of pleasure to tickle a palate cloyed with satiety, and suddenly grown fastidious beyond all measure, so that ordinary pleasures became distasteful. Conscious that at will he was the master of all the women that he could desire, knowing that his power was irresistible, he did not care to exercise it; they were pliant to his unexpressed wishes, to his most extravagant caprices, until he felt a horrible thirst for love, and would have love beyond their power to give.

The world refused him nothing save faith and prayer, the soothing and consoling love that is not of this world. He was obeyed—it was a horrible position.

The torrents of pain, and pleasure, and thought that shook his soul and his bodily frame would have overwhelmed the strongest human being; but in him there was a power of vitality proportioned to the power of the sensations that assailed him. He felt within him a vague immensity of longing that earth could not satisfy. He spent his days on outspread wings, longing to traverse the luminous fields of space to other spheres that he knew afar by intuitive perception, a clear and hopeless knowledge. His soul dried up within him, for he hungered and thirsted after things that can neither be drunk nor eaten, but for which he could not choose but crave. His lips, like Melmoth's, burned with desire; he panted for the unknown, for he knew all things.

The mechanism and the scheme of the world was apparent to him, and its working interested him no longer; he did not long disguise the profound scorn that makes of a man of extraordinary powers a sphinx who knows everything and says nothing, and sees all things with an unmoved countenance. He felt not the slightest wish to communicate his knowledge to other men. He was rich with all the wealth of the world, with one effort he could make the circle of the globe, and riches and power were meaningless for him. He felt the awful melancholy of omnipotence, a melancholy which Satan and

Melmoth Reconciled

God relieve by the exercise of infinite power in mysterious ways known to them alone. Castanier had not, like his Master, the inextinguishable energy of hate and malice; he felt that he was a devil, but a devil whose time was not yet come, while Satan is a devil through all eternity, and being damned beyond redemption, delights to stir up the world, like a dung heap, with his triple fork and to thwart therein the designs of God. But Castanier, for his misfortune, had one hope left.

If in a moment he could move from one pole to the other as a bird springs restlessly from side to side in its cage, when, like the bird, he has crossed his prison, he saw the vast immensity of space beyond it. That vision of the Infinite left him for ever unable to see humanity and its affairs as other men saw them. The insensate fools who long for the power of the Devil gauge its desirability from a human standpoint; they do not see that with the Devil's power they will likewise assume his thoughts, and that they will be doomed to remain as men among creatures who will no longer understand them. The Nero unknown to history who dreams of setting Paris on fire for his private entertainment, like an exhibition of a burning house on the boards of a theatre, does not suspect that if he had the power, Paris would become for him as little interesting as an ant-heap by the roadside to a hurrying passer-by. The circle of the sciences was for Castanier something like a logogriph for a man who does not know the key to it. Kings and Governments were despicable in his eyes. His great debauch had been in some sort a deplorable farewell to his life as a man. The earth had grown too narrow for him, for the infernal gifts laid bare for him the secrets of creation—he saw the cause and foresaw its end. He was shut out from all that men call "heaven" in all languages under the sun; he could no longer think of heaven.

Then he came to understand the look on his predecessor's face and the drying up of the life within; then he knew all that was meant by the baffled hope that gleamed in Melmoth's eyes; he, too, knew the thirst that burned those red lips, and the agony of a continual struggle between two natures grown to giant size. Even yet he might be an angel, and he knew himself to be a fiend. His was the fate of a sweet and gentle creature that a wizard's malice has imprisoned in a

Melmoth Reconciled

mis-shapen form, entrapping it by a pact, so that another's will must set it free from its detested envelope.

As a deception only increases the ardor with which a man of really great nature explores the infinite of sentiment in a woman's heart, so Castanier awoke to find that one idea lay like a weight upon his soul, an idea which was perhaps the key to loftier spheres. The very fact that he had bartered away his eternal happiness led him to dwell in thought upon the future of those who pray and believe. On the morrow of his debauch, when he entered into the sober possession of his power, this idea made him feel himself a prisoner; he knew the burden of the woe that poets, and prophets, and great oracles of faith have set forth for us in such mighty words; he felt the point of the Flaming Sword plunged into his side, and hurried in search of Melmoth. What had become of his predecessor?

The Englishman was living in a mansion in the Rue Ferou, near Saint-Sulpice—a gloomy, dark, damp, and cold abode. The Rue Ferou itself is one of the most dismal streets in Paris; it has a north aspect like all the streets that lie at right angles to the left bank of the Seine, and the houses are in keeping with the site. As Castanier stood on the threshold he found that the door itself, like the vaulted roof, was hung with black; rows of lighted tapers shone brilliantly as though some king were lying in state; and a priest stood on either side of a catafalque that had been raised there.

"There is no need to ask why you have come, sir," the old hall porter said to Castanier; "you are so like our poor dear master that is gone. But if you are his brother, you have come too late to bid him good-bye. The good gentleman died the night before last."

"How did he die?" Castanier asked of one of the priests.

"Set your mind at rest," said the old priest; he partly raised as he spoke the black pall that covered the catafalque.

Castanier, looking at him, saw one of those faces that faith has made sublime; the soul seemed to shine forth from every line of it, bringing light and warmth for other men, kindled by the unfailing charity within. This was Sir John Melmoth's confessor.

"Your brother made an end that men may envy, and that must rejoice the angels. Do you know what joy there is in heaven over a sinner that repents? His tears of penitence, excited by grace, flowed without ceasing; death alone checked them. The Holy Spirit dwelt in him. His burning words, full of lively faith, were worthy of the Prophet-King. If, in the course of my life, I have never heard a more dreadful confession than from the lips of this Irish gentleman, I have likewise never heard such fervent and passionate prayers. However great the measures of his sins may have been, his repentance has filled the abyss to overflowing. The hand of God was visibly stretched out above him, for he was completely changed, there was such heavenly beauty in his face. The hard eyes were softened by tears; the resonant voice that struck terror into those who heard it took the tender and compassionate tones of those who themselves have passed through deep humiliation. He so edified those who heard his words, that some who had felt drawn to see the spectacle of a Christian's death fell on their knees as he spoke of heavenly things, and of the infinite glory of God, and gave thanks and praise to Him. If he is leaving no worldly wealth to his family, no family can possess a greater blessing than this that he surely gained for them, a soul among the blessed, who will watch over you all and direct you in the path to heaven."

These words made such a vivid impression upon Castanier that he instantly hurried from the house to the Church of Saint-Sulpice, obeying what might be called a decree of fate. Melmoth's repentance had stupefied him.

At that time, on certain mornings in the week, a preacher, famed for his eloquence, was wont to hold conferences, in the course of which he demonstrated the truths of the Catholic faith for the youth of a generation proclaimed to be indifferent in matters of belief by another voice no less eloquent than his own. The conference had been put off to a later hour on account of Melmoth's funeral, so Castanier arrived just as the great preacher was epitomizing the proofs of a future existence of happiness with all the charm of eloquence and force of expression which have made him famous. The seeds of divine doctrine fell into a soil prepared for them in the old dragoon, into whom the Devil had glided. Indeed, if there is a phenomenon well attested by experience, is it not the spiritual phenomenon commonly called "the faith of the peasant"? The strength of belief varies inversely with the amount of use that a man has made of his reasoning faculties. Simple people and soldiers belong to the unreasoning class. Those who have marched through life beneath the banner of instinct are far more ready to receive the light than minds and hearts overwearied with the world's sophistries.

Castanier had the southern temperament; he had joined the army as a lad of sixteen, and had followed the French flag till he was nearly forty years old. As a common trooper, he had fought day and night, and day after day, and, as in duty bound, had thought of his horse first, and of himself afterwards. While he served his military apprenticeship, therefore, he had but little leisure in which to reflect on the destiny of man, and when he became an officer he had his men to think of. He had been swept from battlefield to battlefield, but he had never thought of what comes after death. A soldier's life does not demand much thinking. Those who cannot understand the lofty political ends involved and the interests of nation and nation; who cannot grasp political schemes as well as plans of campaign, and combine the science of the tactician with that of the administrator, are bound to live in a state of ignorance; the most boorish peasant in the most backward district in France is scarcely in a worse case. Such men as these bear the brunt of war, yield passive obedience to the brain that directs them, and strike down the men opposed to them as the woodcutter fells timber in the forest. Violent physical exertion is succeeded by times of inertia, when they repair the waste. They fight and drink, fight and eat, fight and sleep, that they may the better deal hard blows; the powers of the mind are not greatly exercised in this turbulent round of existence, and the character is as simple as heretofore.

When the men who have shown such energy on the battlefield return to ordinary civilization, most of those who have not risen to high rank seem to have acquired no ideas, and to have no aptitude, no capacity, for grasping new ideas. To the utter amazement of a younger generation, those who made our armies so glorious and so terrible are as simple as children, and as slow-witted as a clerk at his worst, and the captain of a thundering squadron is scarcely fit to keep a merchant's day-book. Old soldiers of this stamp, therefore being innocent of any attempt to use their reasoning faculties, act upon their strongest impulses. Castanier's crime was one of those matters that raise so many questions, that, in order to debate about it, a moralist might call for its "discussion by clauses," to make use of a parliamentary expression.

Passion had counseled the crime; the cruelly irresistible power of feminine witchery had driven him to commit it; no man can say of himself, "I will never do that," when a siren joins in the combat and throws her spells over him.

So the word of life fell upon a conscience newly awakened to the truths of religion which the French Revolution and a soldier's career had forced Castanier to neglect. The solemn words, "You will be happy or miserable for all eternity!" made but the more terrible impression upon him, because he had exhausted earth and shaken it like a barren tree; because his desires could effect all things, so that it was enough that any spot in earth or heaven should be forbidden him, and he forthwith thought of nothing else. If it were allowable to compare such great things with social follies, Castanier's position was not unlike that of a banker who, finding that his all-powerful millions cannot obtain for him an entrance into the society of the noblesse, must set his heart upon entering that circle, and all the social privileges that he has already acquired are as nothing in his eyes from the moment when he discovers that a single one is lacking.

Here is a man more powerful than all the kings on earth put together; a man who, like Satan, could wrestle with God Himself; leaning against one of the pillars in the Church of Saint-Sulpice, weighed down by the feelings and thoughts that oppressed him, and absorbed in the thought of a Future, the same thought that had engulfed Melmoth.

"He was very happy, was Melmoth!" cried Castanier. "He died in the certain knowledge that he would go to heaven."

In a moment the greatest possible change had been wrought in the cashier's ideas. For several days he had been a devil, now he was nothing but a man; an image of the fallen Adam, of the sacred tradition embodied in all cosmogonies. But while he had thus shrunk he retained a germ of greatness, he had been steeped in the Infinite. The power of hell had revealed the divine power. He thirsted for heaven as he had never thirsted after the pleasures of earth, that are so soon exhausted. The enjoyments which the fiend promises are but the enjoyments of earth on a larger scale, but to the joys of heaven there is no limit. He believed in God, and the spell that gave him the treasures of the world was as nothing to him now; the treasures themselves seemed to him as contemptible as pebbles to an admirer of diamonds; they were but gewgaws compared with the eternal glories of the other life. A curse lay, he thought, on all things that came to him from this source. He sounded dark depths of painful thought as he listened to the service performed for Melmoth. The *Dies irae* filled him with awe; he felt all the grandeur of that cry of a repentant soul trembling before the Throne of God. The Holy Spirit, like a devouring flame, passed through him as fire consumes straw.

The tears were falling from his eyes when—"Are you a relation of the dead?" the beadle asked him.

"I am his heir," Castanier answered.

"Give something for the expenses of the services!" cried the man.

"No," said the cashier. (The Devil's money should not go to the Church.)

"For the poor!"

"No."

"For repairing the Church!"

"No."

"The Lady Chapel!"

"No."

"For the schools!"

"No."

Castanier went, not caring to expose himself to the sour looks that the irritated functionaries gave him.

Melmoth Reconciled

Outside, in the street, he looked up at the Church of Saint-Sulpice. "What made people build the giant cathedrals I have seen in every country?" he asked himself. "The feeling shared so widely throughout all time must surely be based upon something."

"Something! Do you call God *something*?" cried his conscience. "God! God! God!...."

The word was echoed and re-echoed by an inner voice, til it overwhelmed him; but his feeling of terror subsided as he heard sweet distant sounds of music that he had caught faintly before. They were singing in the church, he thought, and his eyes scanned the great doorway. But as he listened more closely, the sounds poured upon him from all sides; he looked round the square, but there was no sign of any musicians. The melody brought visions of a distant heaven and far-off gleams of hope; but it also quickened the remorse that had set the lost soul in a ferment. He went on his way through Paris, walking as men walk who are crushed beneath the burden of their sorrow, seeing everything with unseeing eyes, loitering like an idler, stopping without cause, muttering to himself, careless of the traffic, making no effort to avoid a blow from a plank of timber.

Imperceptibly repentance brought him under the influence of the divine grace that soothes while it bruises the heart so terribly. His face came to wear a look of Melmoth, something great, with a trace of madness in the greatness—a look of dull and hopeless distress, mingled with the excited eagerness of hope, and, beneath it all, a gnawing sense of loathing for all that the world can give. The humblest of prayers lurked in the eyes that saw with such dreadful clearness. His power was the measure of his anguish. His body was bowed down by the fearful storm that shook his soul, as the tall pines bend before the blast. Like his predecessor, he could not refuse to bear the burden of life; he was afraid to die while he bore the yoke of hell. The torment grew intolerable.

At last, one morning, he bethought himself how that Melmoth (now among the blessed) had made the proposal of an exchange, and how that he had accepted it; others, doubtless, would follow his example; for in an age proclaimed, by the inheritors of the eloquence of the Fathers of the Church, to be fatally indifferent to religion, it should be easy to find a man who would accept the conditions of the contract in order to prove its advantages.

"There is one place where you can learn what kings will fetch in the market; where nations are weighed in the balance and systems appraised; where the value of a government is stated in terms of the five-franc piece; where ideas and beliefs have their price, and everything is discounted; where God Himself, in a manner, borrows on the security of His revenue of souls, for the Pope has a running account there. Is it not there that I should go to traffic in souls?"

Castanier went quite joyously on 'Change, thinking that it would be as easy to buy a soul as to invest money in the Funds. Any ordinary person would have feared ridicule, but Castanier knew by experience that a desperate man takes everything seriously. A prisoner lying under sentence of death would listen to the madman who should tell him that by pronouncing some gibberish he could escape through the keyhole; for suffering is credulous, and clings to an idea until it fails, as the swimmer borne along by the current clings to the branch that snaps in his hand.

Towards four o'clock that afternoon Castanier appeared among the little knots of men who were transacting private business after 'Change. He was personally known to some of the brokers; and while affecting to be in search of an acquaintance, he managed to pick up the current gossip and rumors of failure.

"Catch me negotiating bills for Claparon & Co., my boy. The bank collector went round to return their acceptances to them this morning," said a fat banker in his outspoken way. "If you have any of their paper, look out."

Claparon was in the building, in deep consultation with a man well known for the ruinous rate at which he lent money. Castanier went forthwith in search of the said Claparon, a merchant who had a reputation for taking heavy risks that meant wealth or utter ruin. The money-lender walked away as Castanier came up. A gesture betrayed the speculator's despair.

"Well, Claparon, the Bank wants a hundred thousand francs of you, and it is four o'clock; the thing is known, and it is too late to arrange your little failure comfortably," said Castanier.

"Sir!"

"Speak lower," the cashier went on. "How if I were to propose a piece of business that would bring you in as much money as you require?"

"It would not discharge my liabilities; every business that I ever heard of wants a little time to simmer in."

"I know of something that will set you straight in a moment," answered Castanier; "but first you would have to — —"

"Do what?"

"Sell your share of paradise. It is a matter of business like anything else, isn't it? We all hold shares in the great Speculation of Eternity."

"I tell you this," said Claparon angrily, "that I am just the man to lend you a slap in the face. When a man is in trouble, it is no time to pay silly jokes on him."

"I am talking seriously," said Castanier, and he drew a bundle of notes from his pocket.

"In the first place," said Claparon, "I am not going to sell my soul to the Devil for a trifle. I want five hundred thousand francs before I strike — —"

"Who talks of stinting you?" asked Castanier, cutting him short. "You shall have more gold than you could stow in the cellars of the Bank of France."

He held out a handful of notes. That decided Claparon.

"Done," he cried; "but how is the bargain to be make?"

"Let us go over yonder, no one is standing there," said Castanier, pointing to a corner of the court.

Claparon and his tempter exchanged a few words, with their faces turned to the wall. None of the onlookers guessed the nature of this by-play, though their curiosity was keenly excited by the strange gestures of the two contracting parties. When Castanier returned, there was a sudden outburst of amazed exclamation. As in the Assembly where the least event immediately attracts attention, all faces were turned to the two men who had caused the sensation, and

Melmoth Reconciled

a shiver passed through all beholders at the change that had taken place in them.

The men who form the moving crowd that fills the Stock Exchange are soon known to each other by sight. They watch each other like players round a card-table. Some shrewd observers can tell how a man will play and the condition of his exchequer from a survey of his face; and the Stock Exchange is simply a vast card-table. Every one, therefore, had noticed Claparon and Castanier. The latter (like the Irishman before him) had been muscular and powerful, his eyes were full of light, his color high. The dignity and power in his face had struck awe into them all; they wondered how old Castanier had come by it; and now they beheld Castanier divested of his power, shrunken, wrinkled, aged, and feeble. He had drawn Claparon out of the crowd with the energy of a sick man in a fever fit; he had looked like an opium-eater during the brief period of excitement that the drug can give; now, on his return, he seemed to be in the condition of utter exhaustion in which the patient dies after the fever departs, or to be suffering from the horrible prostration that follows on excessive indulgence in the delights of narcotics. The infernal power that had upheld him through his debauches had left him, and the body was left unaided and alone to endure the agony of remorse and the heavy burden of sincere repentance. Claparon's troubles every one could guess; but Claparon reappeared, on the other hand, with sparkling eyes, holding his head high with the pride of Lucifer. The crisis had passed from the one man to the other.

"Now you can drop off with an easy mind, old man," said Claparon to Castanier.

"For pity's sake, send for a cab and for a priest; send for the curate of Saint-Sulpice!" answered the old dragoon, sinking down upon the curbstone.

The words "a priest" reached the ears of several people, and produced uproarious jeering among the stockbrokers, for faith with these gentlemen means a belief that a scrap of paper called a mortgage represents an estate, and the List of Fundholders is their Bible.

"Shall I have time to repent?" said Castanier to himself, in a piteous voice, that impressed Claparon.

A cab carried away the dying man; the speculator went to the bank at once to meet his bills; and the momentary sensation produced upon the throng of business men by the sudden change on the two faces, vanished like the furrow cut by a ship's keel in the sea. News of the greatest importance kept the attention of the world of commerce on the alert; and when commercial interests are at stake, Moses might appear with his two luminous horns, and his coming would scarcely receive the honors of a pun, the gentlemen whose business it is to write the Market Reports would ignore his existence.

When Claparon had made his payments, fear seized upon him. There was no mistake about his power. He went on 'Change again, and offered his bargain to other men in embarrassed circumstances. The Devil's bond, "together with the rights, easements, and privileges appertaining thereunto,"—to use the expression of the notary who succeeded Claparon, changed hands for the sum of seven hundred thousand francs. The notary in his turn parted with the agreement with the Devil for five hundred thousand francs to a building contractor in difficulties, who likewise was rid of it to an iron merchant in consideration of a hundred thousand crowns. In fact, by five o'clock people had ceased to believe in the strange contract, and purchasers were lacking for want of confidence.

At half-past five the holder of the bond was a house-painter, who was lounging by the door of the building in the Rue Feydeau, where at that time stockbrokers temporarily congregated. The house-painter, simple fellow, could not think what was the matter with him. He "felt all anyhow"; so he told his wife when he went home.

The Rue Feydeau, as idlers about town are aware, is a place of pilgrimage for youths who for lack of a mistress bestow their ardent affection upon the whole sex. On the first floor of the most rigidly respectable domicile therein dwelt one of those exquisite creatures whom it has pleased heaven to endow with the rarest and most surpassing beauty. As it is impossible that they should all be duchesses or queens (since there are many more pretty women in the world than titles and thrones for them to adorn), they are content to make a stockbroker or a banker happy at a fixed price. To this good-natured beauty, Euphrasia by name, an unbounded ambition had led a notary's clerk to aspire. In short, the second clerk in the office of Maitre Crottat, notary, had fallen in love with her, as youth at two-and-twenty can fall in love. The scrivener would have murdered the Pope and run amuck through the whole sacred college to procure the miserable sum of a hundred louis to pay for a shawl which had turned Euphrasia's head, at which price her waiting-woman had promised that Euphrasia should be his. The infatuated youth walked to and fro under Madame Euphrasia's windows, like the polar bears in their cage at the Jardin des Plantes, with his right hand thrust beneath his waistcoat in the region of the heart, which he was fit to tear from his bosom, but as yet he had only wrenched at the elastic of his braces.

"What can one do to raise ten thousand francs?" he asked himself. "Shall I make off with the money that I must pay on the registration of that conveyance? Good heavens! my loan would not ruin the purchaser, a man with seven millions! And then next day I would fling myself at his feet and say, 'I have taken ten thousand francs belonging to you, sir; I am twenty-two years of age, and I am in love with Euphrasia—that is my story. My father is rich, he will pay you back; do not ruin me! Have not you yourself been twenty-two years old and madly in love?' But these beggarly landowners have no souls! He would be quite likely to give me up to the public prosecutor, instead of taking pity upon me. Good God! if it were only possible to sell your soul to the Devil! But there is neither a God nor a Devil; it is all nonsense out of nursery tales and old wives' talk. What shall I do?"

"If you have a mind to sell your soul to the Devil, sir," said the house-painter, who had overheard something that the clerk let fall, "you can have the ten thousand francs."

"And Euphrasia!" cried the clerk, as he struck a bargain with the devil that inhabited the house-painter.

The pact concluded, the frantic clerk went to find the shawl, and mounted Madame Euphrasia's staircase; and as (literally) the devil was in him, he did not come down for twelve days, drowning the thought of hell and of his privileges in twelve days of love and riot and forgetfulness, for which he had bartered away all his hopes of a paradise to come.

And in this way the secret of the vast power discovered and acquired by the Irishman, the offspring of Maturin's brain, was lost to mankind; and the various Orientalists, Mystics, and Archaeologists who take an interest in these matters were unable to hand down to posterity the proper method of invoking the Devil, for the following sufficient reasons:

On the thirteenth day after these frenzied nuptials the wretched clerk lay on a pallet bed in a garret in his master's house in the Rue Saint-Honore. Shame, the stupid goddess who dares not behold herself, had taken possession of the young man. He had fallen ill; he would nurse himself; misjudged the quantity of a remedy devised by the skill of a practitioner well known on the walls of Paris, and succumbed to the effects of an overdose of mercury. His corpse was as black as a mole's back. A devil had left unmistakable traces of its passage there; could it have been Ashtaroth?

"The estimable youth to whom you refer has been carried away to the planet Mercury," said the head clerk to a German demonologist who came to investigate the matter at first hand.

"I am quite prepared to believe it," answered the Teuton.

"Oh!"

"Yes, sir," returned the other. "The opinion you advance coincides with the very words of Jacob Boehme. In the forty-eighth proposition of *The Threefold Life of Man* he says that 'if God hath brought all things to pass with a LET THERE BE, the FIAT is the secret matrix which comprehends and apprehends the nature which is formed by the spirit born of Mercury and of God.'"

"What do you say, sir?"

The German delivered his quotation afresh.

"We do not know it," said the clerks.

"*Fiat?*..." said a clerk. "*Fiat lux!*"

"You can verify the citation for yourselves," said the German. "You will find the passage in the *Treatise of the Threefold Life of Man*, page 75; the edition was published by M. Migneret in 1809. It was translated into French by a philosopher who had a great admiration for the famous shoemaker."

"Oh! he was a shoemaker, was he?" said the head clerk.

"In Prussia," said the German.

"Did he work for the King of Prussia?" inquired a Boeotian of a second clerk.

"He must have vamped up his prose," said a third.

"That man is colossal!" cried the fourth, pointing to the Teuton.

That gentleman, though a demonologist of the first rank, did not know the amount of devilry to be found in a notary's clerk. He went away without the least idea that they were making game of him, and fully under the impression that the young fellows regarded Boehme as a colossal genius.

"Education is making strides in France," said he to himself.

PARIS, May 6, 1835.

Melmoth Reconciled

ADDENDUM

The following personages appear in other stories of the Human Comedy.

Aquilina
  The Magic Skin

Claparon, Charles
  A Bachelor's Establishment
  Cesar Birotteau
  The Firm of Nucingen
  A Man of Business
  The Middle Classes

Euphrasia
  The Magic Skin

Nucingen, Baronne Delphine de
  Father Goriot
  The Thirteen
  Eugenie Grandet
  Cesar Birotteau
  Lost Illusions
  A Distinguished Provincial at Paris
  The Commission in Lunacy
  Scenes from a Courtesan's Life
  Modeste Mignon
  The Firm of Nucingen
  Another Study of Woman
  A Daughter of Eve
  The Member for Arcis

Tillet, Ferdinand du
  Cesar Birotteau
  The Firm of Nucingen
  The Middle Classes
  A Bachelor's Establishment

Pierrette
A Distinguished Provencial at Paris
The Secrets of a Princess
A Daughter of Eve
The Member for Arcis
Cousin Betty
The Unconscious Humorists

Copyright © 2022 Esprios Digital Publishing. All Rights Reserved.

CPSIA information can be obtained
at www.ICGtesting.com
Printed in the USA
BVHW041349250523
664860BV00006B/169